I0876916

Social and Emotional Learning Activities

GRADES PreK–K

All illustrations and photography, including those from Shutterstock.com, are protected by copyright.

Writing: Tiffany Rivera
Content Editing: Lisa Vitarisi Mathews
Copy Editing: Laurie Westrich
Art Direction: Yuki Meyer
Cover Design: Yuki Meyer
Illustration: Mary Rojas
Design/Production: Jessica Onken
Paula Acojido

EVAN-MOOR Educational Publishers

EMC 6095

Visit *teaching-standards.com* to view a correlation of this book.

Correlated to Current Standards

Congratulations on your purchase of some of the finest teaching materials in the world.

Photocopying the pages in this book is permitted for single-classroom use only. Making photocopies for additional classes or schools is prohibited.

For information about other Evan-Moor products, call 1-800-777-4362, fax 1-800-777-4332, or visit our website, www.evan-moor.com.
Entire contents © 2021 Evan-Moor Corporation
10 Harris Court, Suite C-3, Monterey, CA 93940-5773. Printed in USA.

004

CPSIA: Sheridan Saline, Inc., Saline, MI, USA [2/2025]

CONTENTS

Introduction

What's in *Social and Emotional Learning Activities*? 4
How to Use This Book 5
About Social and Emotional Learning 6

Activities

Self-Awareness 7
Self-Management 19
Social Awareness 31
Responsible Decision-Making 43
Relationship Skills 55
SEL and Writing 67
SEL and Reading 77
SEL and Math 87
SEL and Social Studies 97

Answer Key 109

What's in *Social and Emotional Learning Activities*?

9 Units of Engaging SEL Activities

Each unit has a different SEL focus and begins with a teacher page. The teacher page has an introduction to read aloud to students and a list of the SEL skills covered in the unit.

The rest of the pages in the unit are reproducible activity pages for students. Some activity pages have a focus box at the top of the page that explains the SEL skill practiced on that page.

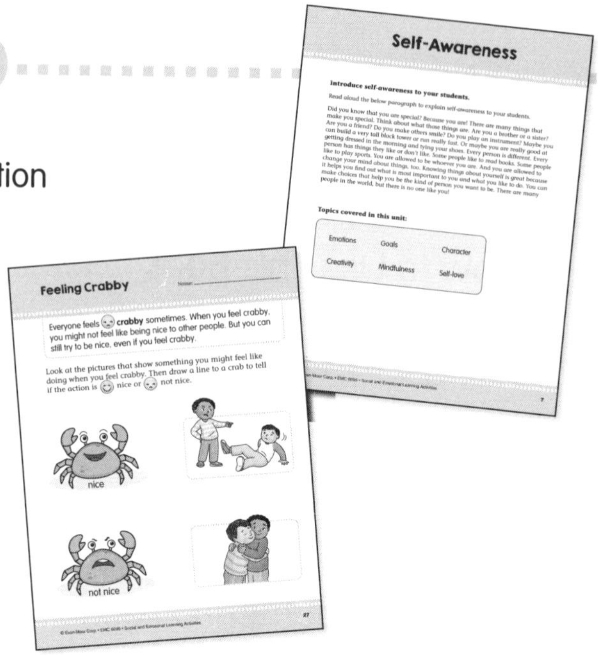

The Activities

The activities are designed to be engaging and open-ended, with a wide variety of response formats. The goal is for students to feel like the activities are providing a “safe space” to let their own unique viewpoint and creativity shine through. For most activities there are no incorrect answers, because each student will have a different worldview and a different set of experiences. Activities include the following:

- tracing and drawing
- mazes and puzzles
- problem solving
- making choices
- critical thinking
- visual information
- art projects

In addition, basic skills such as fine motor skills, visual discrimination, inference, and comprehension are practiced.

Answer Key

For most of the activities in this book, answers will vary. For some activities, a sample answer or correct answer is provided in the answer key section of the book.

How to Use This Book

Planning Instruction

The units in this book and the pages within each unit do not have to be taught in sequential order. Choose the units and/or pages that align with your students' needs.

Note that each unit begins with a teacher page that has an optional introduction to read aloud to students.

The activity pages should be read aloud to students before they begin each activity.

How to Use *Social and Emotional Learning Activities*

Reproduce Each Activity and Distribute It to Students

Have students complete an activity to supplement learning during the school day. Or assign an activity to students as homework.

Use Activities to Guide Whole-Group Discussion

There are different ways to use an activity for a whole-group discussion. You can review student answers as a group after each student completes the activity individually. Or you can use the information in the focus box or the items on the page as a conversation starter.

Use Activities for Small-Group Discussion

Have students talk about their answers and reflect on the activity with a partner or with a small group.

About Social and Emotional Learning

Social and emotional learning (SEL) focuses on the skills we use every day to maintain healthy relationships, manage our behavior, form goals, communicate with others, persevere through challenging situations, reflect on our emotions, and make decisions. One goal of SEL is to empower learners by helping them develop confidence in their own judgment. Research shows that SEL can promote academic and career success. It can also help learners deal with daily stressors.

What Are SEL Skills?

These are some of the skills that are gained and reinforced by SEL:

- empathizing
- making responsible choices
- developing grit
- accepting personal responsibility
- conflict resolution
- setting and achieving goals
- maintaining focus
- mindfulness
- constructive communication
- evaluating possible outcomes
- monitoring self-talk
- developing healthy coping methods
- demonstrating flexibility
- optimistic thinking
- cooperation
- monitoring expectations

Evan-Moor's Approach to SEL

The activities in this book are designed to be culturally responsive and considerate of the cultural diversity found in the classroom and in the world around us. The messaging in this book seeks to avoid labeling any feelings as *wrong* or *bad*. Instead, we appeal to students' abilities to think creatively, critically, reflectively, and empathically. We believe that SEL skills can be practiced and applied in daily life.

Self-Awareness

Introduce self-awareness to your students.

Read aloud the below paragraph to explain self-awareness to your students.

Did you know that you are special? Because you are! There are many things that make you special. Think about what those things are. Are you a brother or a sister? Are you a friend? Do you make others smile? Do you play an instrument? Maybe you can build a very tall block tower or run really fast. Or maybe you are really good at getting dressed in the morning and tying your shoes. Every person is different. Every person has things they like or don't like. Some people like to read books. Some people like to play sports. You are allowed to be whoever you are. And you are allowed to change your mind about things, too. Knowing things about yourself is great because it helps you find out what is most important to you and what you like to do. You can make choices that help you be the kind of person you want to be. There are many people in the world, but there is no one like you!

Topics covered in this unit:

Emotions	Goals	Character
Creativity	Mindfulness	Self-love

I Am Special

Name: ____________________

I am special. There is no one like me.

1. Finish the sentence.

My name is

____________________.

2. Draw a picture of yourself.

3. Write a number to finish the sentence.
Then draw the same number of candles  on the cake.

I am ____________ years old.

When I Grow Up

Name: ______________________

I can be whoever I want to be.

1. There are many different jobs. Circle the pictures that show a job that looks fun to do.

chef

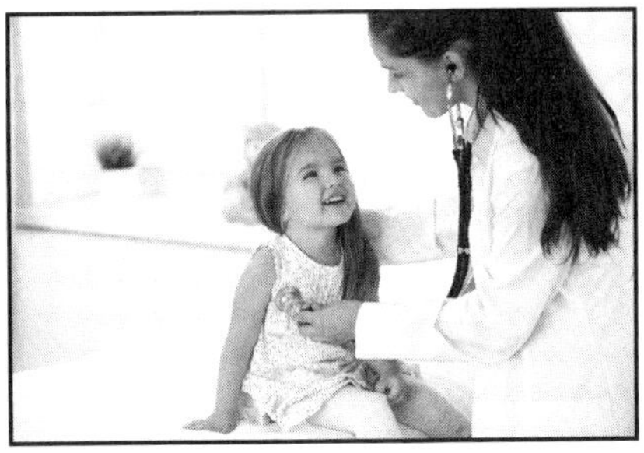

doctor

athlete

firefighter

teacher

2. Draw a picture of yourself doing the job you want to do when you grow up.

© Evan-Moor Corporation • EMC 6095 • Social and Emotional Learning Activities

Things I Can Do

Name: ____________________

I am good at many things.

Circle the pictures that show what you are good at.

singing

dancing

drawing

playing a sport

playing an instrument

being a friend

I Do It Best

Name: ____________________

I am good at many things.

1. Draw a picture of what you do best.

2. Color the face that shows how you feel when you do the activity you drew.

mad sad happy sleepy silly

© Evan-Moor Corporation

More Practice

Name: ____________________

There are some things I am not good at.
But I can ask for help and practice to get better.

Circle the pictures to show which activities you would like to be better at.

reading

tying my shoes

playing an instrument

playing a sport

riding a bike

drawing

Many Kinds of Feelings

Name: ____________________

People have many kinds of feelings.
Sometimes you like how you feel.
Sometimes you do not like how you feel.

Draw a picture in each part of the circle. Draw what you think about each feeling. Use different colors.

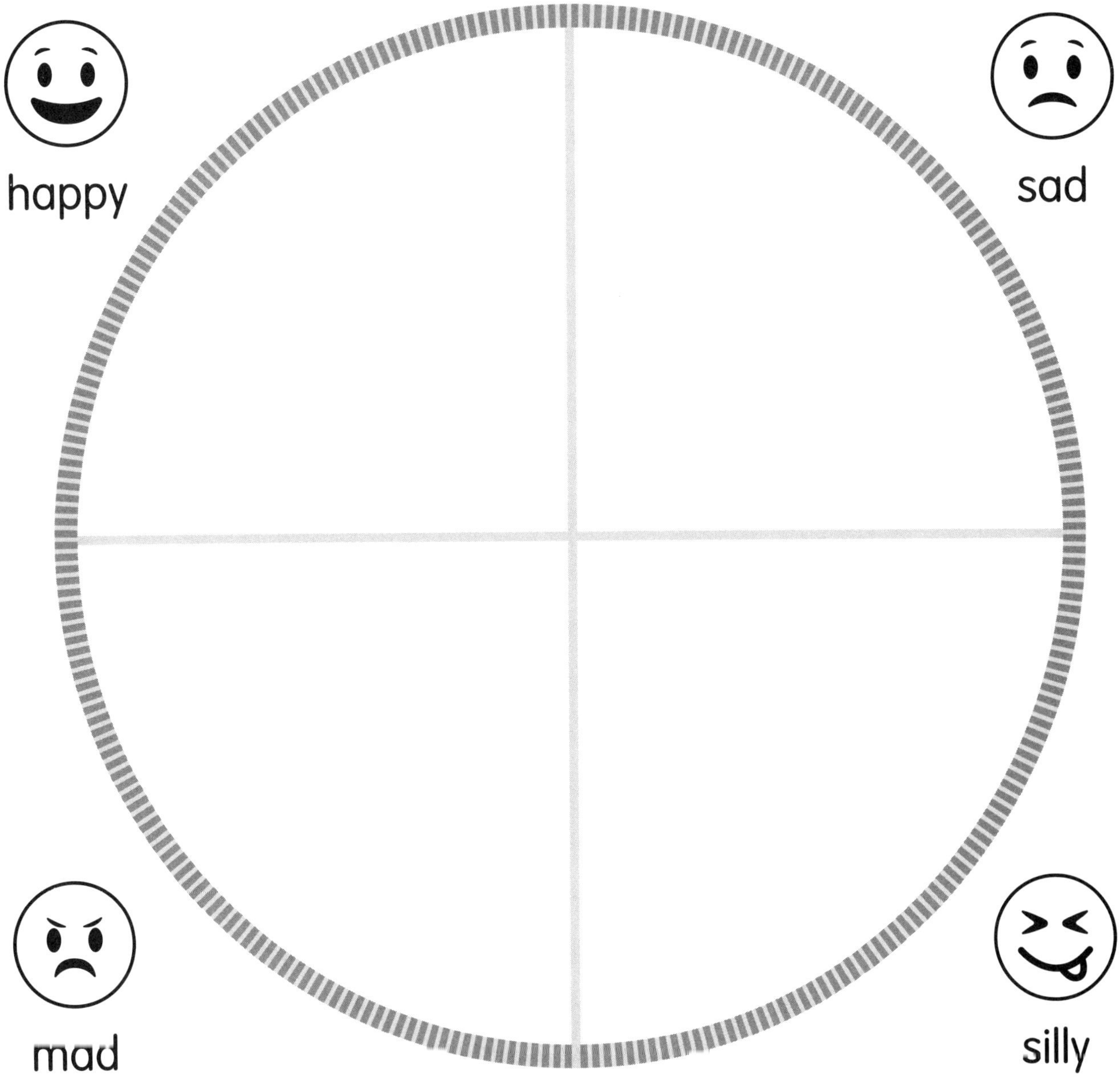

Feelings Change

Name: ____________________

People's feelings can change. People can feel

For one week, at the end of each day, draw a face to show how you felt.

Sunday	Monday	Tuesday	Wednesday
Thursday	**Friday**	**Saturday**	**Notes**

I Love Me

Name: ____________________

I am special. There is no one like me. I love me!

Color the picture.

My Self-Portrait

Name: ___________________________

I am special. There is no one like me.

Make a paper plate look just like you.

What You Need

- paper plate
- paint, crayons, or marker
- optional: beads, pasta, yarn, buttons, beans, glue, etc.

What You Do

1. Color or paint a paper plate to look like the color of your skin. Let the paint dry.
2. Color or use what you have to make hair, eyes, a nose, a mouth, and ears. Make the paper plate look like your face.
3. Then show your paper plate to a friend.

Self-Management

Introduce self-management to your students.

Read aloud the below paragraph to explain self-management to your students.

There are many different types of feelings. You can be happy, sad, mad, nervous, surprised, and many others. People, things, and events can make you feel different feelings. You choose how to act when you feel your feelings. You can choose what you do and say. You can choose to be kind to others. You can choose to follow the rules. But what about when you feel unhappy? Sometimes it is hard to be nice to others when you are unhappy. You might feel like being mean to other people. Or you might feel like not following the rules. It is okay to not feel happy all the time. But you can still make good choices, even if you are unhappy. There are many things you can do to try to feel better. You can snuggle with a soft blanket or toy. You can find a quiet place to sit, close your eyes, and take deep breaths. And you can always tell someone you trust how you feel. Remember that you have people who love you and will keep you safe.

Topics covered in this unit:

Emotions	Mindfulness	Fear
Empathy	Self-talk	Coping skills

Butterfly Patterns

Name: ____________________

Some people feel good when they draw.
Some people like to draw patterns.

Draw to match the pattern on the butterfly wing.

1.

2.

3. Now draw your own pattern.

Social and Emotional Learning Activities • EMC 6095 • © Evan-Moor Corporation

Furry Friend

Name: ____________________

Pets can help you feel better when you are

mad,

sad,

or scared.

Pets who are funny and playful can make people laugh.

Color by number to find the furry pet.

1 purple   2 blue   3 yellow   4 orange

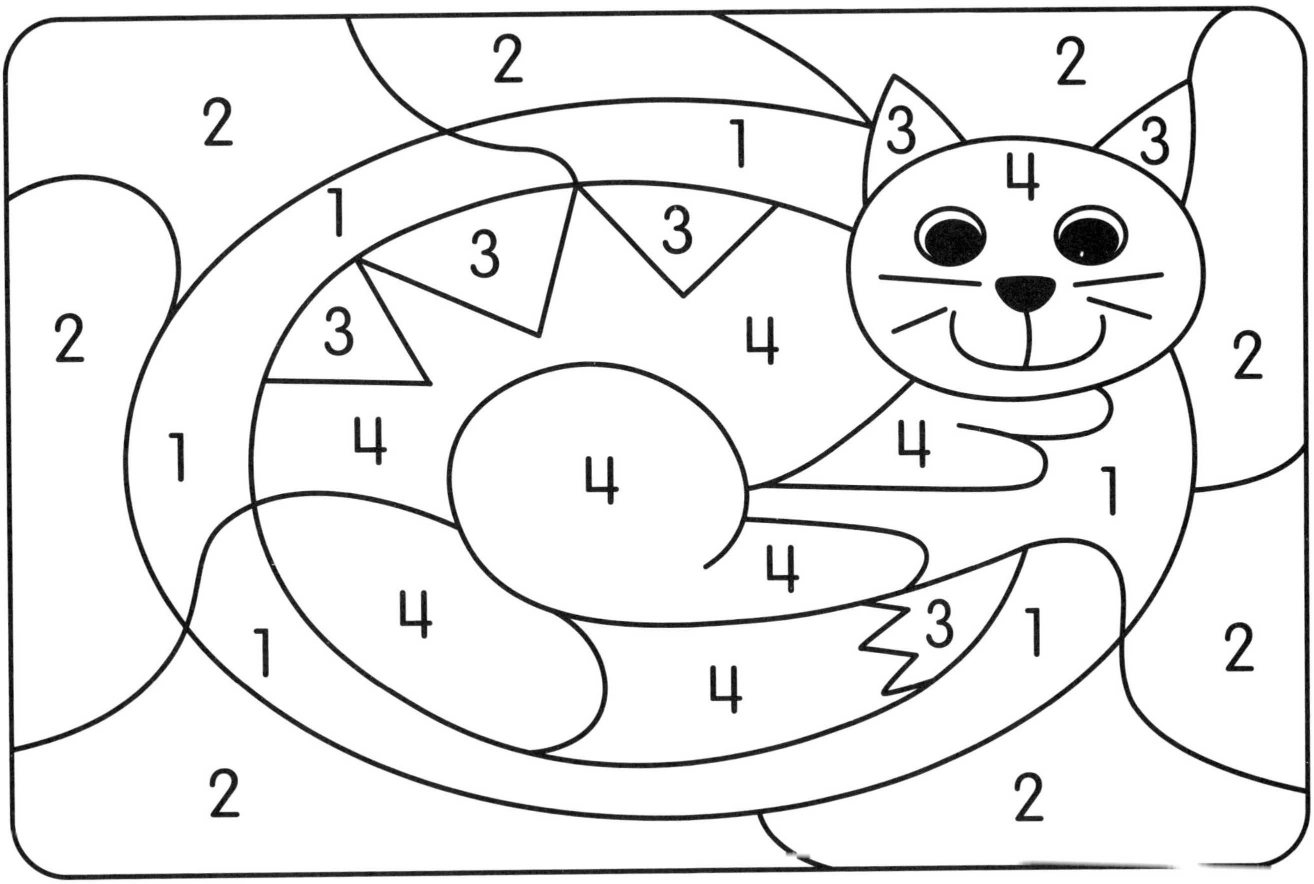

Roar Like a Lion

Name: ______________________

Some things can make you feel so **mad** that you want to yell or roar loudly like a lion. But you can use a quiet voice to tell someone how you feel.

1. Draw a picture of something that makes you mad and want to roar like a lion.

2. Draw a picture of someone you can talk to when you feel mad.

Social and Emotional Learning Activities • EMC 6095 • © Evan-Moor Corporation

Count to Ten

Name: ____________________

Everyone feels **mad** sometimes. But you can stop, take deep breaths, and count from 1 to 10 to feel better.

Count out loud as you connect the dots. Then color the picture.

I Can Feel Better

Name: ______________________

Fear is a feeling. All people feel fear or get scared sometimes. When you feel scared, you can do things to feel better.

1. Draw a picture of a time you felt scared.

2. Circle the picture or pictures that would make you feel better when you feel scared.

Hold a soft toy

Read a book

Hug someone

Social and Emotional Learning Activities • EMC 6095 • © Evan-Moor Corporation

Feeling Crabby

Name: ______________________

Everyone feels **crabby** sometimes. When you feel crabby, you might not feel like being nice to other people. But you can still try to be nice, even if you feel crabby.

Look at the pictures that show something you might feel like doing when you feel crabby. Then draw a line to a crab to tell if the action is nice or not nice.

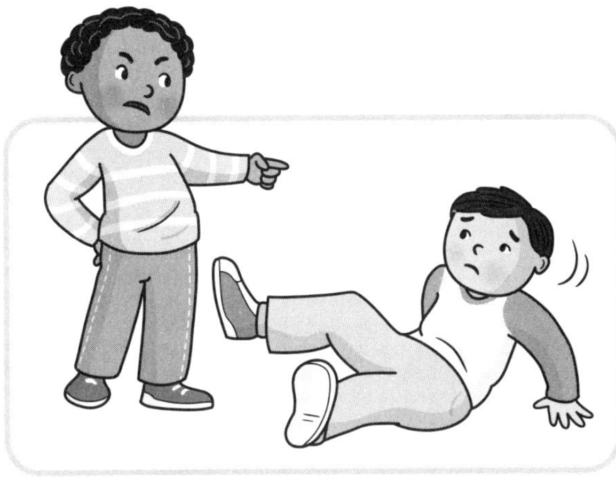

Happy Thoughts

Name: ______________________

Did you know happy thoughts can make people feel happy? Try to have happy thoughts as much as you can!

Trace the word to finish the sentence.
Then read the sentence out loud.

I am smart.

I am kind.

I am loved.

Feelings and the Weather

Name: ______________________

Feelings are like the weather. They change.

One day you can feel  happy.

The next day you can feel  sad.

Look at each weather picture. Think about how it makes you feel. Then color the picture.

Some Bunny to Hold

Name: ______________________

Some people like to hold a soft toy when they feel  sad.

You can make a stuffed bunny to hold when you want to feel better.

What You Need

- sock
- cotton balls
- rubber bands
- scissors
- markers

What You Do

1. First, fill a sock with cotton balls.
2. Next, put a rubber band around the sock. This is the bunny's body.
3. Now make the bunny's head. Fill the part above the rubber band with cotton balls and put a rubber band around it. Make sure to leave enough of the sock to make the bunny's ears.
4. Now, cut the top of the sock in half to make two ears.
5. Finally, decorate your bunny by drawing eyes, a nose, and a mouth.

Social and Emotional Learning Activities • EMC 6095 • © Evan-Moor Corporation

Social Awareness

Introduce social awareness to your students.

Read aloud the below paragraphs to explain social awareness to your students.

Everyone feels sad sometimes. Everyone feels happy sometimes. Everyone has feelings. Sometimes you can guess how someone feels by looking at the person's face. You can guess how a person feels by looking at the way he or she moves his or her body. Some people have a big smile when they feel happy. Some people jump up and down when they feel excited. Some people will have a frown on their face and fold their arms when they feel mad.

Sometimes you and a friend will not feel the same way about things. And that is okay. But it is important to treat every person with respect. This means it is important to treat people the way you want to be treated. One way to show a person respect is to listen carefully to him or her. It is important to listen when a friend says, "No," "Stop," or "I don't like that." You can also show a person respect by being kind. The things you do can sometimes make people feel sad, mad, or happy. If your friend is sad, you can do things to help him or her feel better.

Topics covered in this unit:

Emotions	Inclusion	Empathy
Body language	Communication	Cultural differences

Faces and Feelings

Name: ____________________

People's faces show feelings.

Trace the feeling words. Then color the pictures.

happy

sad

mad

surprised

scared

excited

Social and Emotional Learning Activities • EMC 6095 • © Evan-Moor Corporation

Feelings Show

Name: ____________________________

People's faces show feelings.

Look at the picture. Draw a line to the word that tells how you think the child feels.

happy

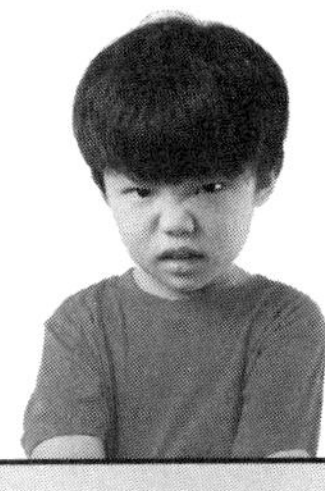

mad

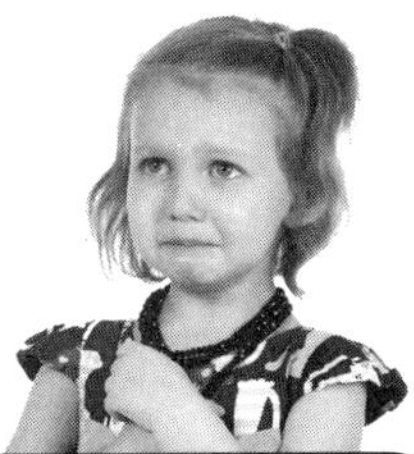

sad

surprised

How Does He Feel?

Name: ______________________________

People's faces show feelings.

Look at the picture. Answer the items.

1. Color the face that shows how the boy feels.

 happy

 sad

sleepy

2. Fill in the circle below the picture that shows why the boy is sad.

○

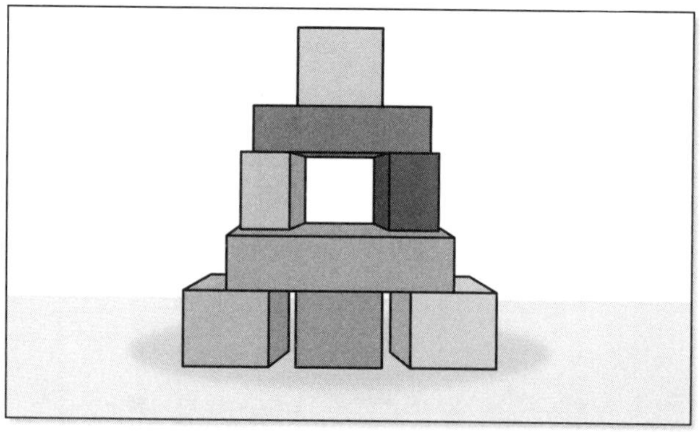

○

Play with Me

Name: ______________________

If you see a person playing alone, you can ask him or her to play with you. It will make the person feel happy. It will make you feel happy, too!

Draw a line through the maze to play with a new friend.

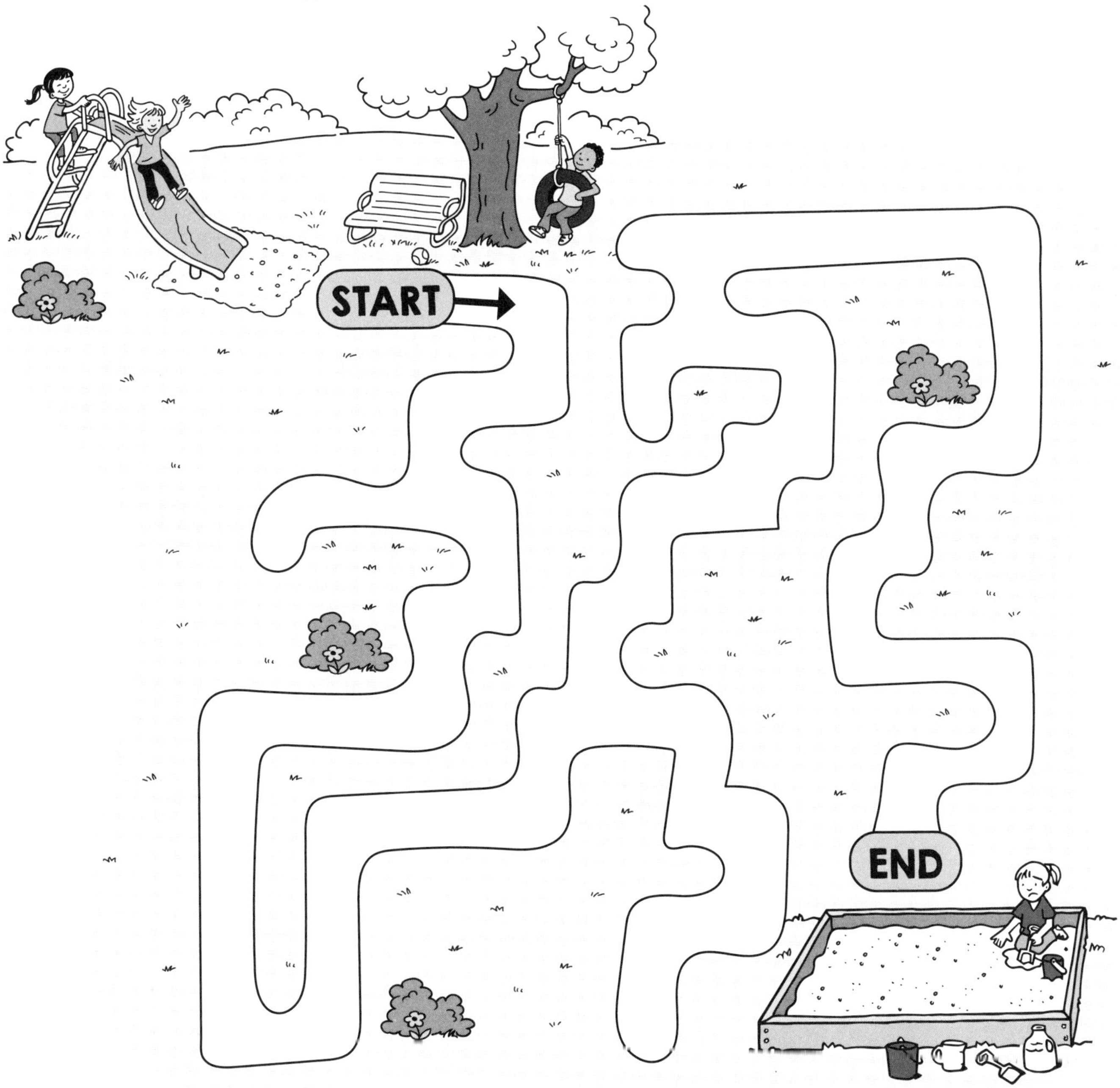

Feel Better

Name: ______________________

You can make a friend feel better when he or she feels sad.

1. Oh no! Yung-Ai hurt her finger.

   Color the face that shows how she feels.

    sad    happy

2. Circle the picture that will make Yung-Ai feel better.

laugh

help

Social and Emotional Learning Activities • EMC 6095 • © Evan-Moor Corporation

Use Your Words

Name: ______________________

Sometimes a friend will use words to tell you how he or she feels. It is important to listen to the words your friend says.

Look at the picture.
Trace **yes** if both friends want to play together.
Trace **no** if both friends do not want to play together.

no

yes

no

Show How They Feel

Name: ____________________

People sometimes feel

happy

sad

mad

surprised

Look at the pictures. Draw an emoji face next to each picture to show how the child feels.

Cheer Up

Name: ______________________

Sometimes people feel sad. But you can do things to help make people feel better.

Trace the line to help make each friend feel better.

Say Hello

Name: ______________________

Different people say hello in different ways.

Color each picture that shows how some people say hello.

wave

bow

hug

fist bump

Pets Have Feelings

Name: ____________________

People and pets have feelings. A pet uses its face and body to show how it feels.

Look at each pet. Read the words. Cut and glue the faces from page 42 to show how each pet feels.

1. 

sad

glue

2. 

happy

glue

3. 

surprised

glue

Pets Have Feelings,
continued

Name: ______________________

4.

mad

glue

5.

sleepy

glue

Responsible Decision-Making

Introduce responsible decision-making to your students.

Read aloud the below paragraph to explain responsible decision-making to your students.

Sometimes it is easy to know the right thing to do. And sometimes it is not easy to choose what to do. Sometimes it is not easy to be kind when you feel mad. But being kind is always a good choice. You can choose to be a friend. You can choose to help. You can choose to be kind. It is important to treat others how you want them to treat you. Before you do something, stop and think. Is what I am about to do safe? Is it kind? Will it hurt myself or others? Thinking before you do something can help you make good choices.

Topics covered in this unit:

Respect	Mindfulness	Responsibility
Self-awareness	Emotions	Healthy habits
Rules	Self-talk	Environmental awareness

I Choose to Be Kind

Name: ______________________________

I make good choices. I choose to be kind.

Look at the picture.

Color ☺ if it is kind. Color ☹ if it is not kind.

All Done Playing

Name: ______________________

I make good choices. I put my toys away when I am done playing with them.

Help put the toys away. Cut out the pictures below and glue them in the correct toy box.

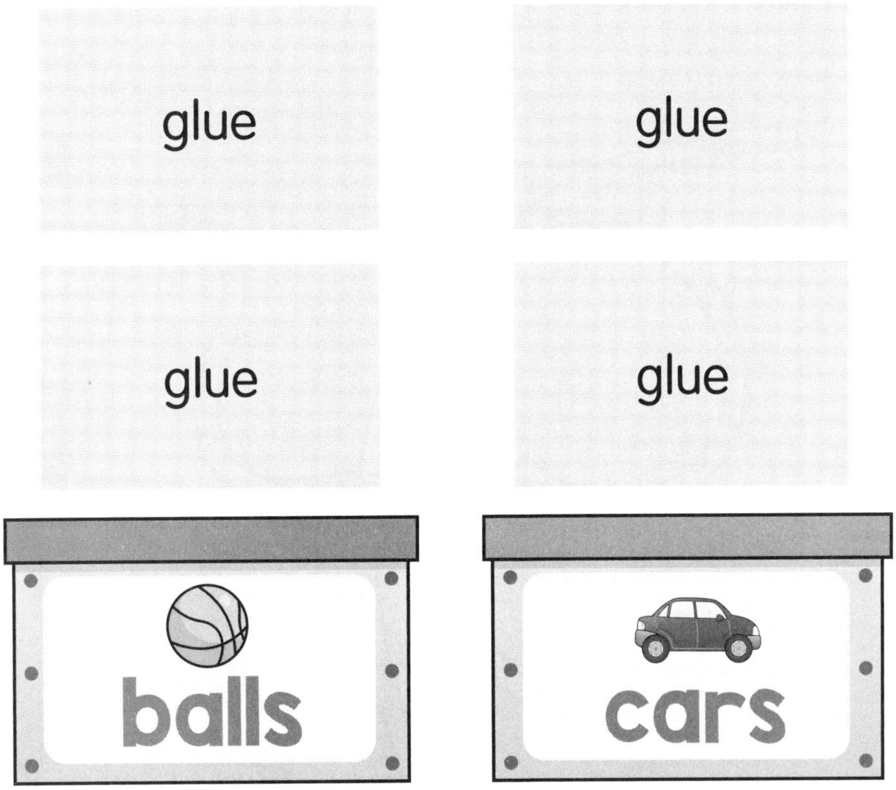

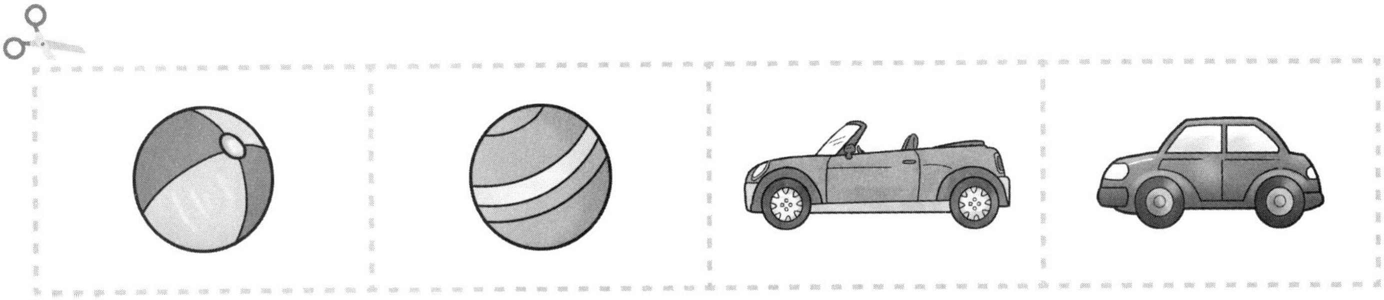

No More Germs

Name: ______________________

I make good choices that keep germs away. I wash my hands.
I cover my mouth when I sneeze. I clean up my mess.

Trace the lines to give each child what he or she needs.

Social and Emotional Learning Activities • EMC 6095 • © Evan-Moor Corporation

Washing Hands

Name: ______________________

I make good choices. I wash my hands before and after I eat. I wash my hands after I play. I wash my hands after I use the bathroom.

Write **1**, **2**, **3**, and **4** to show how to wash your hands.

Wet hands and get soap.

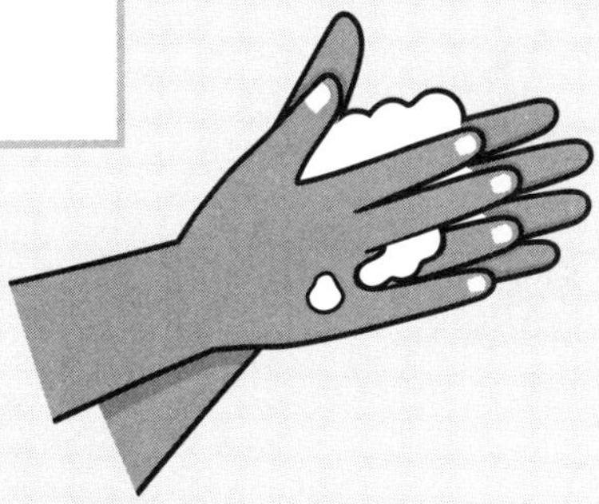

Wash for 20 seconds.

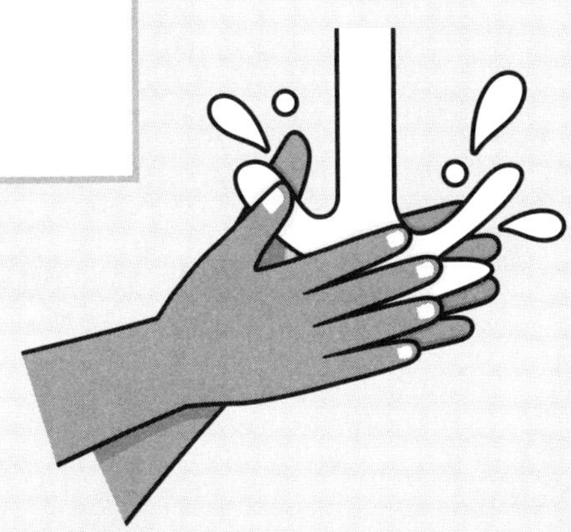

Rinse your hands with clean water.

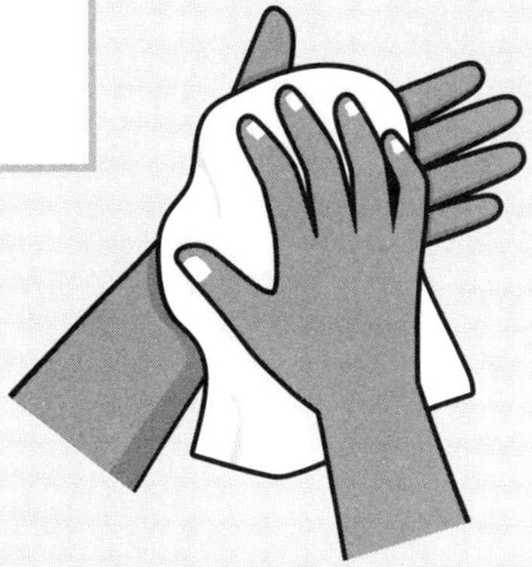

Dry your hands.

Healthy Choices

Name: ______________________________

I make healthy choices.

Circle the pictures that show what you like to do to be healthy.

 © Evan-Moor Corporation

Cross the Street

Name: ____________________

I make good choices. I follow the rules.

Look at the picture. Trace the word.

go

stop

Look at the picture. Is it a good choice?

Color for yes or for no.

Feel Better

Name: ____________________

Sometimes it is not easy being kind to others when you feel mad. But being kind is always a good choice.

Draw a picture to show what you can do to feel better.

When I feel  sad or  mad, I can

tell someone how I feel.

do things that make me happy.

Take Care of the Earth

Name: ____________________

The things I do matter, so I make good choices.
I help take care of the Earth.

Look at the picture. Is it good for the Earth?

Color for yes or for no.

yes no

yes no

yes no

yes no

I Can Do It!

Name: ______________________

Sometimes it can be hard to make the right choice. But you can do it! You can choose to make good choices every day.

Color the picture.

Super Helpers

Name: ______________________________

You can choose to help people and be a good friend.

Make a mask and a friendship bracelet for you and a friend to show that you both choose to be super helpers!

What You Need

- masks on page 54
- crayons or markers
- scissors
- string
- hole punch
- glue

What You Do

1. Color then cut out the masks on page 54.
2. Next, use a hole punch to make a hole in each end of the masks. Then pull the string through the holes and tie the string in a knot.
3. Next, color and cut out the friendship bracelets.
4. Finally, put on your masks and bracelets and act like super helpers!

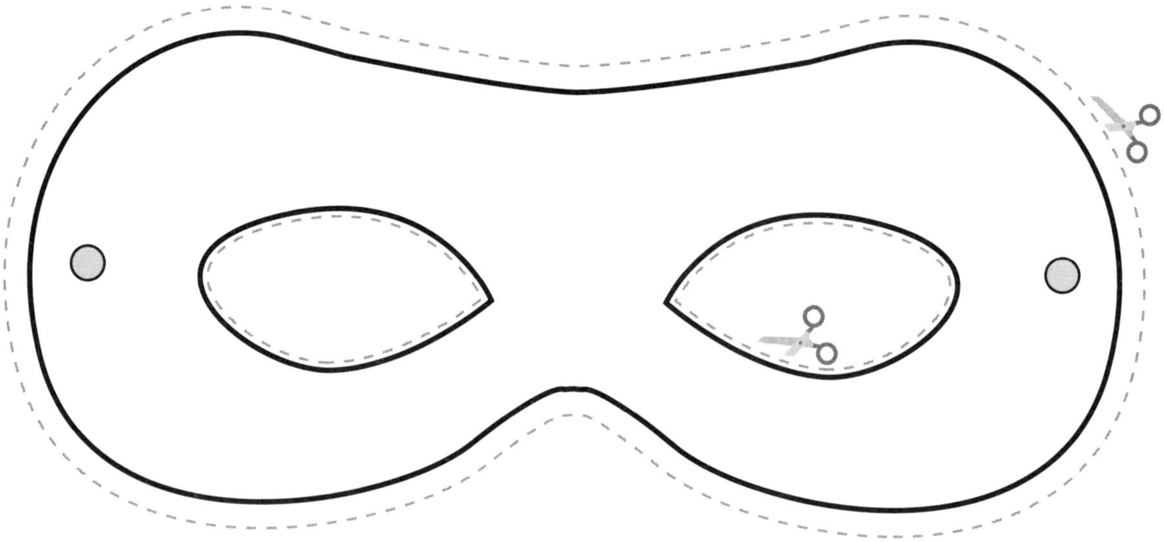

glue
glue

Relationship Skills

Introduce relationship skills to your students.

Read aloud the below paragraphs to explain relationship skills to your students.

There are many people who love you and care about you. Think about who those people are. Do you love them and care about them, too?

Think about how you show your friends and family that you love them. One way to show people you care is to treat them the way you want to be treated. You can say nice words like *please, thank you, I'm sorry,* and *excuse me*. You can show people you love them by smiling at them, listening when they speak, or sharing your toys.

Sometimes you might have a problem with someone you love. Maybe your friend does not want to play the same game as you do. Maybe your friend does not like the same foods as you do. But that's okay. People can like different things and still be friends.

Topics covered in this unit:

Respect	Kindness	Helping others
Taking turns	Empathy	Friendship
Problem solving		

Nice Words

Name: ____________________

I know how to be a good friend. I say nice words.

Read the poem to the tune of "Twinkle, Twinkle, Little Star."

I say "thank you," I say "please,"
When I get help with what I need.

I say "I'm sorry" when I find,
I do something that's not so kind.

I also say "excuse me," too,
When I need to talk or move past you.

Trace the nice words.

please

thank you

I'm sorry

excuse me

Sharing Is Caring

Name: ____________________

I know how to be a good friend. I share.

Rondo wants to share his apples with his friends.
Draw a line to give each friend an apple.

Friendship Words

Name: ____________________

Friends help. Friends play. Friends do things to make each other feel better, like giving a hug.

Look at the words that tell about friendship. Then find and circle them in each box.

help

f h e l p m

play

p l a y d s

hug

x t p h u g

Taking Turns

Name: ______________________

Taking turns can be hard. Sometimes you have to wait. Sometimes a friend has to wait. But taking turns gives everyone a chance to play.

1. Look at each picture. Color 👍 if they are taking turns or 👎 if they are not.

2. Color the face that shows how you feel when a friend does not want to share or take turns with you.

Same and Different

Name: ____________________

Sometimes friends like the same things. Sometimes friends do not like the same things. People can like different things and still be friends!

Color the picture green if you like it.
Color the picture yellow if your friend likes it.
Color the picture blue if you and your friend both like it.

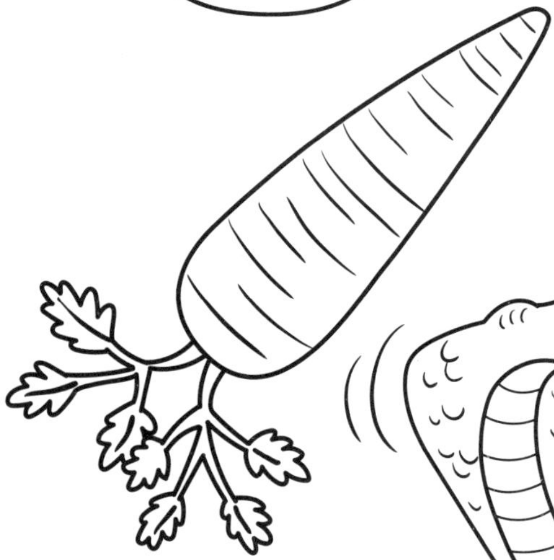

Friendship Garden

Name: ____________________

Friendships are like flowers. Flowers grow when you take care of them and give them the things they need. You can do things to help your friendships grow, too.

You can show friends you like them by doing kind things. Color a flower each time you do something kind for a friend.

You Are My Sunshine

Name: ____________________

A good friend makes you feel warm and happy when you feel sad. Just like when the sun shines on a cold, dark day.

Color and cut out each sun. Then give it to someone who makes you feel warm and happy.

I Love You Beary Much!

Name: ____________________

Make a bear card for someone you love.

What You Need

- cutouts from page 66
- a pencil
- crayons or markers
- scissors
- glue

What You Do

1. Write the name of the person you love on the line on the bear card on page 66.
2. Color the bear card and the front and back of the bear arms.
3. Cut out the bear card and the bear arms.
4. Glue the arms to the back of the card.
5. Fold the arms in front of the card on the dotted lines.
6. Give your card to someone you love.

Name: ____________________

SEL and Writing

Introduce SEL and writing to your students.

Read aloud the below paragraphs to explain SEL and writing to your students.

Sometimes people use words to say what they think or how they feel. Sometimes people write words that tell how they feel, too.

You can write a letter to tell a person how you feel.

You can write nice words in a card for a friend.

Sometimes writing a silly story can make you feel happy when you feel sad or mad. Try it!

Topics covered in this unit:

Respect	Kindness	Body language
Friendship	Emotions	

I Use Nice Words

Name: ______________________

The words you say to people can make them feel good or bad. You can choose to use nice words.

Look at the picture.
Trace the nice word to make a sentence.

You are funny.

It is pretty!

You are a good friend.

What Are They Thinking?

Name: ______________________

People's faces and bodies show feelings.

Sometimes friends show you how they feel or what they think. Draw a line to match the word with the picture. Then trace the word.

stop •

• 

help •

• 

yes •

• 

Say How I Feel

Name: ____________________

It is important to tell people how you feel.

Trace the feeling word. Then draw a picture to show a time when a friend did something that made you feel happy or sad.

I felt happy when

I felt sad when

© Evan-Moor Corporation

My Silly Rhyme

Name: ____________________

Sometimes you can feel silly. Sometimes saying a silly rhyme can make you feel happy.

Trace the word in each sentence. Write a word from the box that rhymes with the word you traced. Then color the animal.

hat	rug
pot	log

The blue dog is on a ____________.

The red cat has on a ____________.

Good Choices

Name: ____________________

Put your pencil on **START HERE**. Then follow the line with your pencil. When you get to a letter, write it on a line in the sentence below. The letters will spell a word to finish the sentence.

I make ____ ____ ____ ____ choices.

Social and Emotional Learning Activities • EMC 6095 • © Evan-Moor Corporation

Play Time Letters

Name: ______________________________

Find the letter that matches the number. Write the letter in the box to help Carmelo ask Gina a question.

1 = a	2 = e	3 = l
4 = m	5 = p	6 = y

Will you ☐ ☐ ☐ ☐ with ☐ ☐ ?

5 3 1 6   4 2

I Am a Star

Name: ____________________

Draw a picture of yourself in the big star. Trace the words that tell about you. Then color the picture.

Good Friend Card

Name: ____________________

Make a card for a good friend.

What You Need

- a sheet of construction paper
- cutouts on page 76
- crayons or markers
- scissors
- glue

What You Do

1. Fold the sheet of construction paper in half so that it opens like a birthday card.
2. Color the picture and words on page 76. Cut them out. Glue them onto the front of the card.
3. Cut out the letter on page 76. On the top line, write the name of the person you will give the card to. Next, trace the words to tell your friend how he or she makes you feel. Then write your name at the bottom of the letter.
4. Glue the letter on the inside of the card.
5. Use crayons or markers to draw pictures on the card.
6. Last, give the card to your good friend.

Good Friend Card, continued

Name: ____________________

Good Friends!

Dear ____________________,

You are a good friend.

You make me happy.

From,

____

your name

Social and Emotional Learning Activities • EMC 6095 • © Evan-Moor Corporation

SEL and Reading

Introduce SEL and reading to your students.

Read aloud the below paragraphs to explain SEL and reading to your students.

Did you know that reading a book can make you feel better when you feel mad or sad? You should try it! Pick a book and find a quiet and comfy place to read.

Some books have a story inside. A story tells you about a person, place, or thing. A story can tell you about pretend things. A story can also tell you about real things that have happened. When you read a story, think about the people or characters in the story. How do they feel? Why do they feel that way?

Some stories tell about how other people might feel. Some stories show how you might feel sometimes, too. Some stories can show you how to make good choices and how to be kind to your friends, family, and things around you. Some stories show you not-so-good choices so you can learn not to make those same mistakes.

Reading a story can help you learn about other people and about yourself.

Topics covered in this unit:

Inclusion	Kindness	Emotions
Making friends	First day of school	Communication
Social awareness		

First Day of School

Name: ____________________

Read the story.

Today is the first day of school.

I say "Hi" to my teacher.

I say "Goodbye" to Mom and Dad.

I want to play. But I feel sad.

Puja says, "Do you want to play?"

I say "Yes!"

We play. We read.

We have fun.

I love school!

Social and Emotional Learning Activities • EMC 6095 • © Evan-Moor Corporation

First Day of School, continued

Name: ______________________

I know how to be a good friend. I share.

Look at the picture.
Circle the face that shows how the boy felt in the story.

Time to Play

Name: ____________________

Read the story.

It is time to play!

Ana likes to play in the sandbox.

Sam likes to play ball.

"Do you want to play ball with me?" Sam asks Ana.

"No, thank you," says Ana.

Sam kicks down Ana's sand house and walks away.

Time to Play,
continued

Name: ______________________

Answer the items about the story you read.

1. Draw a face that shows how Ana feels at the end of the story.

2. Color the face to show how Sam feels when Ana does not want to play.

3. Sam kicked down Ana's sand house. Was this a good choice?

   Color  if it was a good choice.

   Color  if it was not a good choice.

Reading with Friends

Name: ____________________

Reading with friends can make you happy.

Draw a picture of a book you want to read with a friend. Then color the picture.

Social and Emotional Learning Activities • EMC 6095 • © Evan-Moor Corporation

A Quiet and Comfy Place

Name: ____________________

When you feel **mad** or **sad**, you can find a quiet place to read. Reading in a quiet, comfy place can make you feel better.

Answer the items.

1. Circle the pictures that show a comfy place where you would like to read a book.

2. Draw a picture of your favorite place to read a book.

My Feelings Book

Name: ______________________

Cut on the dotted lines. Fold on the solid lines to make a book. Then read each page and draw a picture.

I feel sad.

I feel happy.

fold

fold

I feel mad.

I have many feelings.

SEL and Math

Introduce SEL and math to your students.

Read aloud the below paragraph to explain SEL and math to your students.

Doing math is easy for some people. For other people, it is hard to do. But that is okay. Every person has things they are good at and things they are not as good at. Just try your best! You will get better with each try. When a math problem seems too hard, stop and take a deep breath. Tell yourself, "I can do it!" Then try again. You can always ask for help, too.

Topics covered in this unit:

Self-care	Caring	Mindfulness
Helping others	Self-awareness	Healthy habits
Environmental awareness		

Quiet Place

Name: ______________________

Some people like to spend time in a quiet place.

Color the number 1 to help the girl find a quiet place to read.

START		1	1	1	1	3	7
4	6	8	2	5	1	4	9
9	1	1	1	1	1	6	3
5	1	2	6	7	9	8	4
7	1	1	1	1	1	END	

Social and Emotional Learning Activities • EMC 6095 • © Evan-Moor Corporation

I Love My Pet

Name: ____________________

Pets can make you feel **happy** when you feel **sad**.
You can do things to make your pets happy, too.

Draw a line to give each pet 1 bowl of food.

Count the Helpers

Name: ____________________

I can help keep the Earth clean.

Look at the picture. Count how many kids are helping in the park. Then write the number in the box.

Mindful Coloring

Name: ____________________

Some people like how they feel when they color a picture.

Think about how you feel as you color by number.

1 red   2 green   3 yellow   4 blue

© Evan-Moor Corporation • EMC 6095 • Social and Emotional Learning Activities

Helpful Shapes

Name: ____________________

You can do nice things for other people.
Helping people makes you feel good.

Draw a line to the shape the friend used to help.

Shake It

Name: ______________________

Dancing is a fun way to move your body and stay healthy. Dancing can make you feel happy.

Follow the directions to make your own dance.

What You Need

- dance die pattern on page 96
- numbered die
- glue
- scissors

What You Do

1. Have a grownup cut out the dance die pattern on page 96 and glue the tabs together to make a die.
2. Roll the dance die. This shows you the dance move you will do. Then roll your numbered die. This shows how many times to do the dance move.
3. Take turns rolling the dice with a friend to move your body and have fun dancing!

Shake It, continued

Name: ______________________

Social and Emotional Learning Activities • EMC 6095 • © Evan-Moor Corporation

SEL and Social Studies

Introduce SEL and social studies to your students.

Read aloud the below paragraph to explain SEL and social studies to your students.

The world is big. It is filled with land, water, plants, animals, and people. In some places the weather changes with the seasons. But in some places, like the Arctic, it is always cold. How is the weather where you live? Do you live in a small town? Or do you live in a busy city? Do you think the people in your town can make you feel loved, cared for, and safe? A good neighbor can make you feel all those things. A good neighbor is kind. A good neighbor keeps his or her town clean and safe. A good neighbor helps people. A good neighbor loves and cares for others, even people who are different from themselves. Did you know that people come from many different places in the world? Each person is different. But there are many ways we are the same. Every person needs food, water, and a safe place to live. Every person deserves love, respect, and kindness.

Topics covered in this unit:

Good citizenship	Community helpers	Seasons
Habitats	Cultural differences	Feelings
What living things need		

Community Helpers

Name: ______________________

Community helpers are people who work where you live.
Community helpers do work to help others.

Trace the line from each community helper to the car he or she uses to help others.

I Am a Good Neighbor

Name: ________________________________

Good neighbors are kind. Good neighbors help. Good neighbors do things to help their town stay safe and clean.

Color  if the person is being a good neighbor.

Color  if the person is not being a good neighbor.

Keep It Clean

Name: ______________________

I help keep the Earth clean.

Help the children clean up the park.

Draw a line through the maze to pick up the trash and throw it in the trash bin.

Seasons

Name: ____________________

In many places around the world, the weather changes with the seasons.

What does each season look like where you live?

Draw a picture that shows what you like to do during each season. Be sure to show the weather, too.

Spring	Summer
Fall	**Winter**

Would You Live Here?

Name: ______________________

There are many different habitats in the world. Some deserts have very hot weather. In the Arctic, it is always cold.

Look at the picture of each habitat. Color it.

Then write **yes** or **no** under the picture to tell if you would like to live in the habitat.

Desert	Arctic

______________________	______________________

What I Need

Name: ______________________________

People need some things to live and grow. People need food, water, and a safe place to live. There are some things people want and like, but do not need.

Color things red that you need to live and grow.

Color things blue that you do not need, but you want.

© Evan-Moor Corporation • EMC 6095 • Social and Emotional Learning Activities

Same But Different

Name: ____________________

There are children all over the world. They are just like you. They have friends. They have family. They like to have fun, too.

Draw a line to match the pictures that show kids doing the same thing in a different way.

kids eating together

kids playing

family celebrating

Inside a Piñata

Name: ____________________

A piñata is a colorful shape filled with candy, fruit, and small toys. People hit the piñata until the treats fall out. Piñatas were first used a long time ago in China, Italy, and Spain. Now many people around the world use a piñata for fun.

What are your favorite treats or small toys? Draw 3 things that you would like to fall out of a piñata.

It's a Small World

Name: ______________________

There are many people around the world. Each person is different. But there are many ways we are the same, too. Every person is special. Every person is important.

Color the picture.

Play Your Feelings

Name: ____________________

A djembe is a drum from West Africa. This drum is played for many reasons. It can be played for fun or to celebrate special days. It is played when something sad happens, too.

You can make a djembe and play it to show how you feel.

What You Need

- 2 paper cups
- plastic bag
- rubber band
- cutouts on page 108
- crayons
- string
- scissors
- tape
- glue

What You Do

1. Have a grownup cut the bottom out of both cups. Then tape the two cups together at the bottom of each cup.
2. Cut a circle out of a plastic bag and stretch it over the top of one end of the cups. Use a rubber band to hold it in place.
3. Cut out and color the patterns on page 108. Glue them to each cup.
4. Use string to decorate one end of your drum.
5. Then play your drum to show how you feel.

Play Your Feelings, continued

Name: ____________________

Answer Key

Many of the activities in this book are not included in the answer key because answers vary based on each student's perspective and life experience.

Page 20

Page 25

Page 27

Page 33

Page 34

Page 35

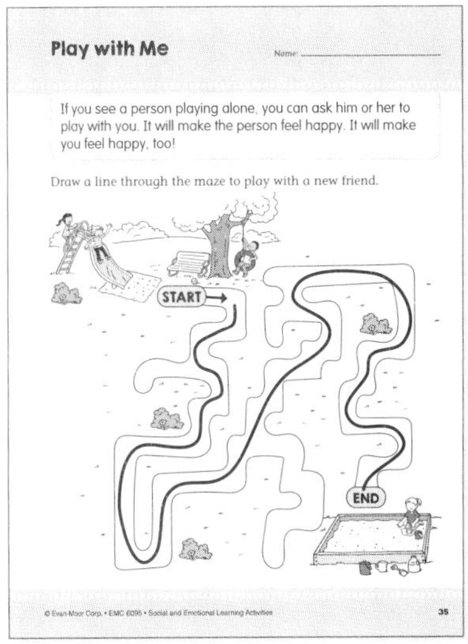

Page 36

Page 38

Page 41

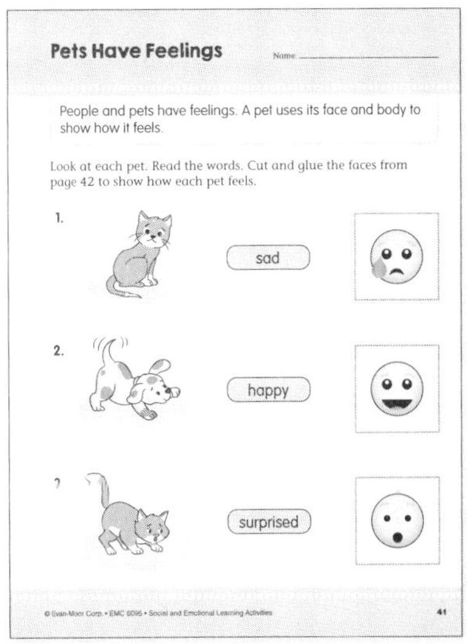

Page 42

Pets Have Feelings, continued

Name:

4. mad

5. sleepy

Page 44

I Choose to Be Kind

Name:

I make good choices. I choose to be kind.

Look at the picture.

Color ☺ if it is kind. Color ☹ if it is not kind.

Page 45

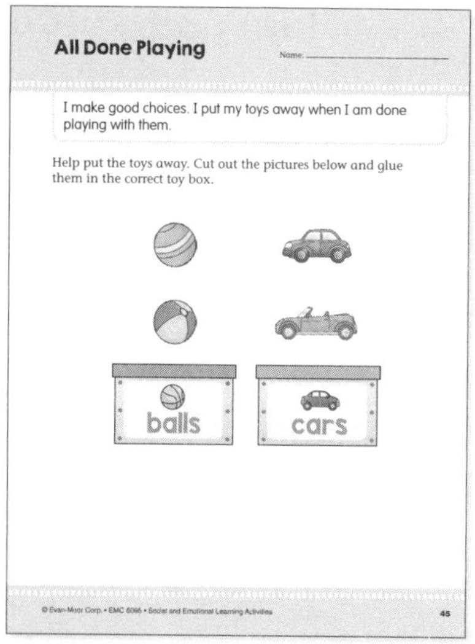

All Done Playing

Name:

I make good choices. I put my toys away when I am done playing with them.

Help put the toys away. Cut out the pictures below and glue them in the correct toy box.

balls

cars

Page 47

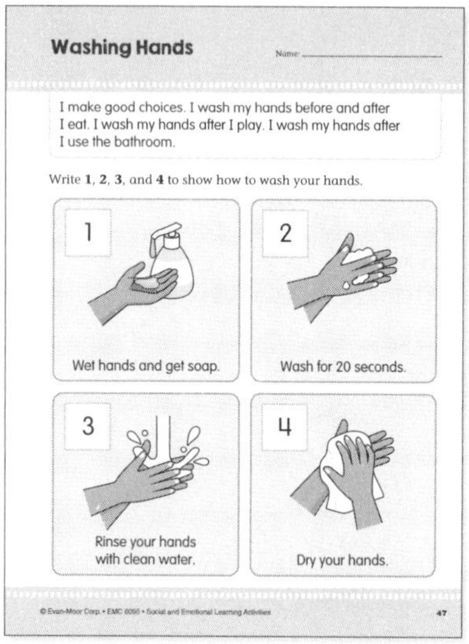

Washing Hands

Name:

I make good choices. I wash my hands before and after I eat. I wash my hands after I play. I wash my hands after I use the bathroom.

Write **1**, **2**, **3**, and **4** to show how to wash your hands.

1 Wet hands and get soap.

2 Wash for 20 seconds.

3 Rinse your hands with clean water.

4 Dry your hands.

Page 49

Cross the Street

Name:

I make good choices. I follow the rules.

Look at the picture. Trace the word.

go

stop

Look at the picture. Is it a good choice?

Color 👍 for yes or 👎 for no.

Page 51

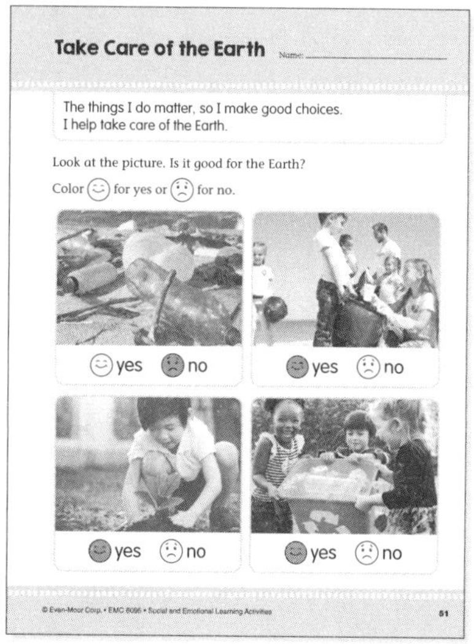

Take Care of the Earth

Name:

The things I do matter, so I make good choices. I help take care of the Earth.

Look at the picture. Is it good for the Earth?

Color ☺ for yes or ☹ for no.

yes no

yes no

yes no

yes no

Page 57

Sharing Is Caring

Name:

I know how to be a good friend. I share.

Rondo wants to share his apples with his friends. Draw a line to give each friend an apple.

Page 60

Friendship Words

Name:

Friends help. Friends play. Friends do things to make each other feel better, like giving a hug.

Look at the words that tell about friendship. Then find and circle them in each box.

help — helpn

play — plays

hug — xthug

Page 61

Taking Turns

Name:

Taking turns can be hard. Sometimes you have to wait. Sometimes a friend has to wait. But taking turns gives everyone a chance to play.

1. Look at each picture. Color 👍 if they are taking turns or 👎 if they are not.

2. Color the face that shows how you feel when a friend does not want to share or take turns with you. Answers will vary.

Page 69

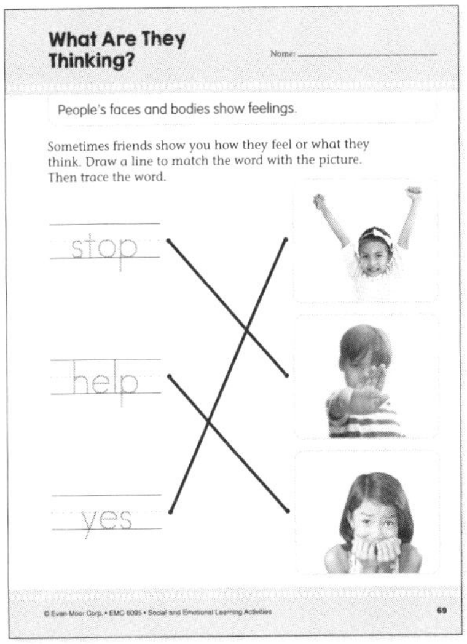
What Are They Thinking? Name: ______

People's faces and bodies show feelings.

Sometimes friends show you how they feel or what they think. Draw a line to match the word with the picture. Then trace the word.

stop

help

yes

© Evan-Moor Corp. • EMC 6095 • Social and Emotional Learning Activities 69

Page 71

My Silly Rhyme Name: ______

Sometimes you can feel silly. Sometimes saying a silly rhyme can make you feel happy.

Trace the word in each sentence. Write a word from the box that rhymes with the word you traced. Then color the animal.

hat rug pot log

The blue dog is on a log.

The red cat has on a hat.

© Evan-Moor Corp. • EMC 6095 • Social and Emotional Learning Activities 71

Page 72

Good Choices Name: ______

Put your pencil on **START HERE**. Then follow the line with your pencil. When you get to a letter, write it on a line in the sentence below. The letters will spell a word to finish the sentence.

START HERE

I make g o o d choices.

72 Social and Emotional Learning Activities • EMC 6095 • © Evan-Moor Corp.

Page 73

Play Time Letters Name: ______

Find the letter that matches the number. Write the letter in the box to help Carmelo ask Gina a question.

1 = a 2 = e 3 = l

4 = m 5 = p 6 = y

Will you p l a y with m e ?

© Evan-Moor Corp. • EMC 6095 • Social and Emotional Learning Activities 73

Page 79

First Day of School, continued Name: ______

I know how to be a good friend. I share. NO AK

Look at the picture.
Circle the face that shows how the boy felt in the story.

© Evan-Moor Corp. • EMC 6095 • Social and Emotional Learning Activities 79

Page 81

Time to Play, continued Name: ______

Answer the items about the story you read.

Drawings will vary.

1. Draw a face that shows how Ana feels at the end of the story.

2. Color the face to show how Sam feels when Ana does not want to play.

3. Sam kicked down Ana's sand house. Was this a good choice?
Color 👍 if it was a good choice.
Color 👎 if it was not a good choice.

© Evan-Moor Corp. • EMC 6095 • Social and Emotional Learning Activities 81

Page 83

Rainy Day, continued Name: ______

Answer the items about the poem you read.

1. Draw a picture of the weather to show why the girl is sad.
Drawings will vary.

2. Circle the picture that shows one thing the girl wants to do.

3. Draw a face to show how you feel when it rains outside.

© Evan-Moor Corp. • EMC 6095 • Social and Emotional Learning Activities 83

Page 88

Quiet Place Name: ______

Some people like to spend time in a quiet place.

Color the number 1 to help the girl find a quiet place to read.

START	1	1	1	1	3	7
4	6	8	2	5	1	4	9
9	1	1	1	1	1	6	3
5	1	2	6	7	9	8	4
7	1	1	1	1	1	END

88 Social and Emotional Learning Activities • EMC 6095 • © Evan-Moor Corp.

Page 89

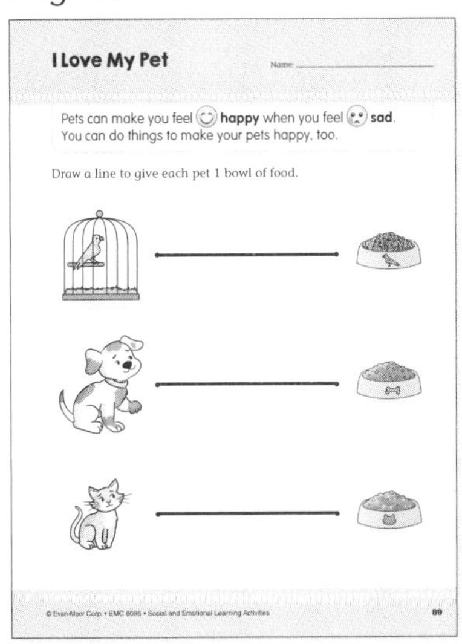
I Love My Pet Name: ______

Pets can make you feel happy when you feel sad. You can do things to make your pets happy, too.

Draw a line to give each pet 1 bowl of food.

© Evan-Moor Corp. • EMC 6095 • Social and Emotional Learning Activities 89

Page 90

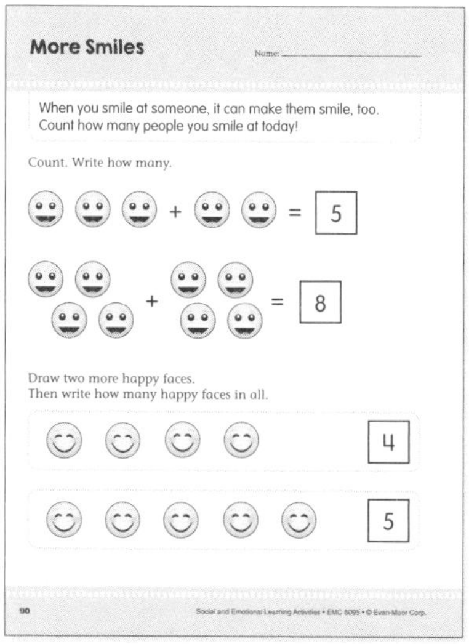

More Smiles

Name: ______________

When you smile at someone, it can make them smile, too. Count how many people you smile at today!

Count. Write how many.

Draw two more happy faces. Then write how many happy faces in all.

90 Social and Emotional Learning Activities • EMC 6095 • © Evan-Moor Corp.

Page 92

Count the Helpers

Name: ______________

I can help keep the Earth clean.

Look at the picture. Count how many kids are helping in the park. Then write the number in the box.

92 Social and Emotional Learning Activities • EMC 6095 • © Evan-Moor Corp.

Page 94

Helpful Shapes

Name: ______________

You can do nice things for other people. Helping people makes you feel good.

Draw a line to the shape the friend used to help.

94 Social and Emotional Learning Activities • EMC 6095 • © Evan-Moor Corp.

Page 99

I Am a Good Neighbor

Name: ______________

Good neighbors are kind. Good neighbors help. Good neighbors do things to help their town stay safe and clean.

Color 👍 if the person is being a good neighbor.
Color 👎 if the person is not being a good neighbor.

© Evan-Moor Corp. • EMC 6095 • Social and Emotional Learning Activities 99

Page 100

Keep It Clean

Name: ______________

I help keep the Earth clean.

Help the children clean up the park.

Draw a line through the maze to pick up the trash and throw it in the trash bin.

100 Social and Emotional Learning Activities • EMC 6095 • © Evan-Moor Corp.

Page 103

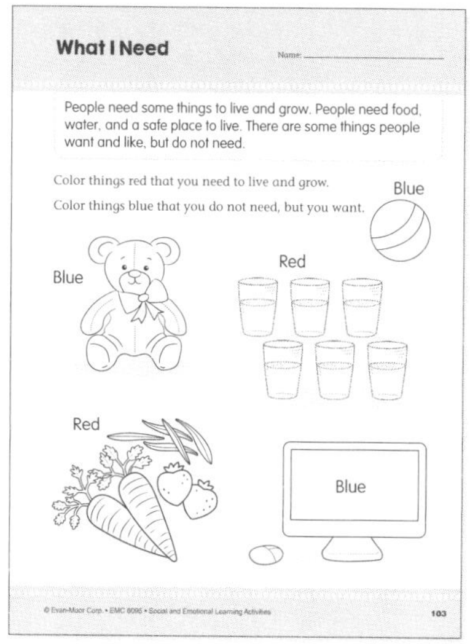

What I Need

Name: ______________

People need some things to live and grow. People need food, water, and a safe place to live. There are some things people want and like, but do not need.

Color things red that you need to live and grow.
Color things blue that you do not need, but you want.

© Evan-Moor Corp. • EMC 6095 • Social and Emotional Learning Activities 103

Page 104

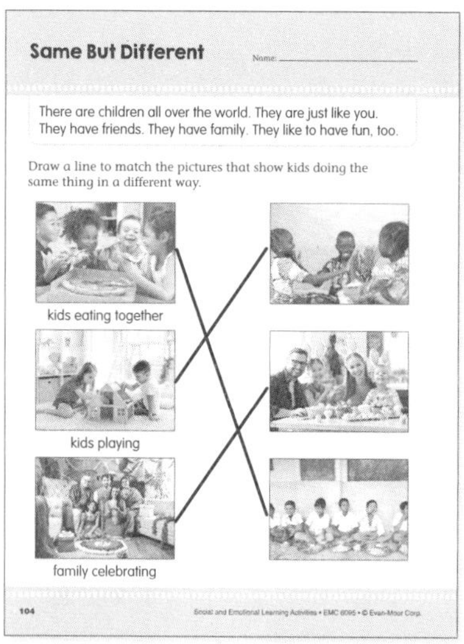

Same But Different

Name: ______________

There are children all over the world. They are just like you. They have friends. They have family. They like to have fun, too.

Draw a line to match the pictures that show kids doing the same thing in a different way.

104 Social and Emotional Learning Activities • EMC 6095 • © Evan-Moor Corp.